To my little monsters
Kade, Bryer, and Dodge;
I love you!
- Mommy

For Eli, Logan, Ashley,
Ryan, Saraya, Mom, Ty,
and Dad for giving me equal
parts inspiration, honesty,
grief, and endless support.
-NA

Library of Congress Catalog Card Number: 2012911546
ISBN-13: 978-1478113171
ISBN-10: 1478113170

story by
saraya
Evenson

Pictures by
Nicholas
Adkins

The
Great
Big
Scary
Monster

The great big scary monster

with the silly green face

Lives in the
corner of
the woods,

in his cavey place

He ROMPS

and

STOMPS

and TROMPS

THROUGH MUD

It squishes

in his toes

He never blows his nose

He steps on
every flower

and climbs up every tree

He really likes to make a mess

but *that* doesn't bother me

He can make
up funny
Songs

and he plays
a mean
kazoo

He'll do anything for a laugh,

He can jump

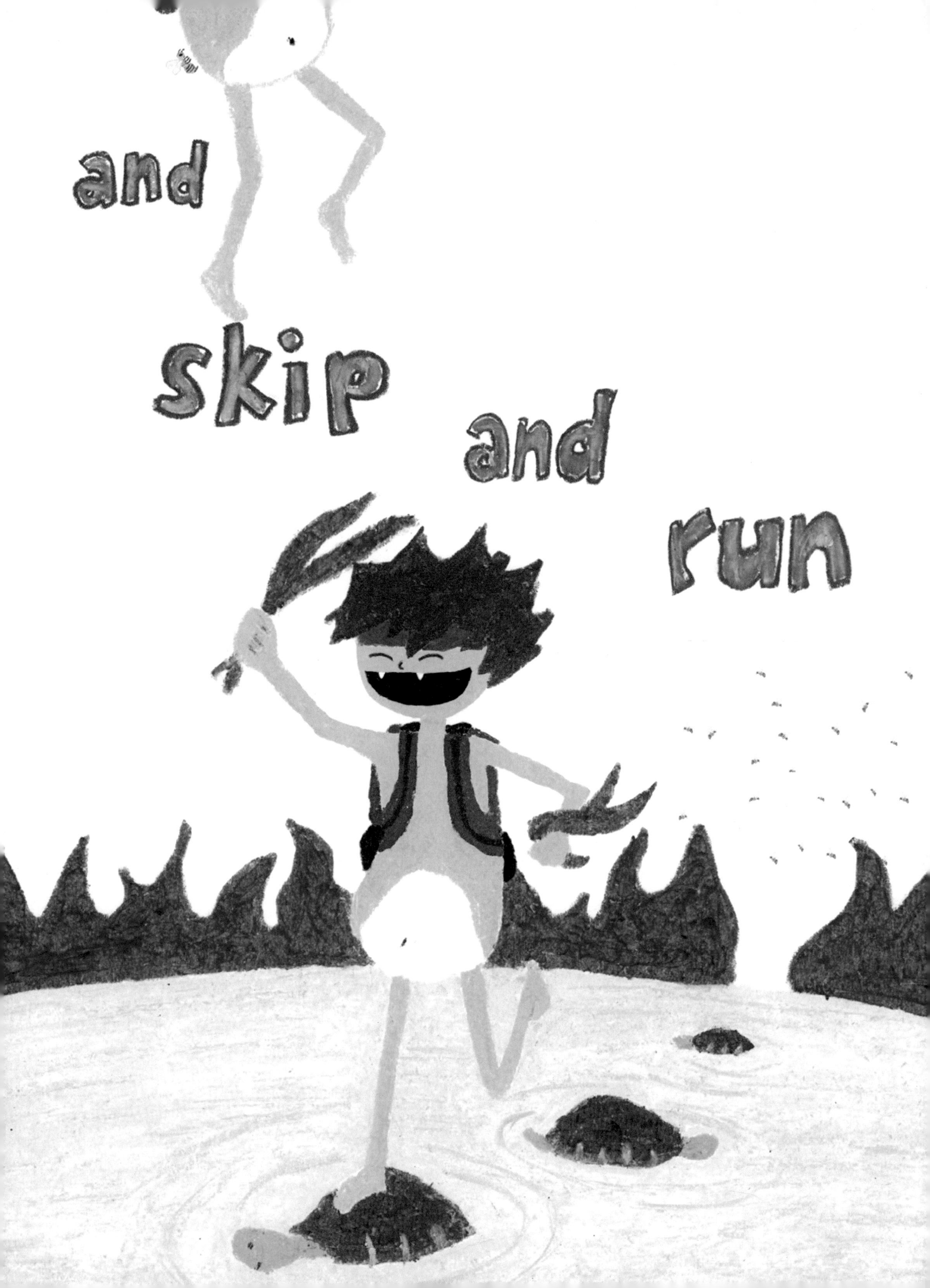
and
skip
and
run

And when it comes down to it, he's really very fun!

And what I
like the very
best
is you're
MINE,
MINE,
MINE!

95478825R00020